ALFIE
GIVES A HAND

Shirley Hughes

RED FOX

One day Alfie came home from Nursery
School with a card in an envelope. His best
friend, Bernard, had given it to him.

ALFIE GIVES A HAND

For Jamie and Henry

Alfie stories in Red Fox

ALFIE GETS IN FIRST

ALFIE'S FEET

ALFIE GIVES A HAND

AN EVENING AT ALFIE'S

THE BIG ALFIE AND ANNIE ROSE STORYBOOK

THE BIG ALFIE OUT OF DOORS STORYBOOK

RHYMES FOR ANNIE ROSE

A Red Fox Book

Published by Random House Children's Books
20 Vauxhall Bridge Road, London SW1V 2SA
A division of The Random House Group Ltd
London Melbourne Sydney Auckland
Johannesburg and agencies throughout the world
Copyright © Shirley Hughes 1983
7 9 10 8
First published in Great Britain by
The Bodley Head Children's Books 1983
This Red Fox edition 1997
All rights reserved
Printed in Hong Kong
THE RANDOM HOUSE GROUP Ltd Reg. No. 954009
www.randomhouse.co.uk
ISBN 0 09 925607 X

"Look, it's got my name on it," said
Alfie, pointing.
Mum said that it was an invitation to
Bernard's birthday tea party.

"Will it be at Bernard's house?" Alfie wanted to know. He'd never been there before. Mum said yes, and she told him all about birthday parties, and how you had to take a present, and about the games and how there would be nice things to eat.

Alfie was very excited about Bernard's party. When the day came Mum washed Alfie's face and brushed his hair and helped him put on a clean T-shirt and his brand-new shorts.

"You and Annie Rose are going to be at the party, too, aren't you?" asked Alfie.

"Oh, no," said Mum. "I'll take you to Bernard's house and then Annie Rose and I will go to the park and come back to collect you when it's time to go home."

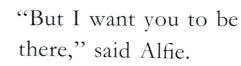

"But I want you to be there," said Alfie.

Mum told him that she and Annie Rose hadn't been invited to the party, only Alfie, because he was Bernard's special friend.

"You don't mind my leaving you at Nursery School, do you?" she said. "So you won't mind being at Bernard's house either, as soon as you get there."

Mum had bought some crayons for Alfie to give Bernard for his birthday present. While she was wrapping them up, Alfie went upstairs. He looked under his pillow and found his old bit of blanket which he kept in bed with him at night.

He brought it downstairs, and sat down to wait for Mum.

"You won't want your old blanket at the party," said Mum, when it was time to go.

But Alfie wouldn't leave his blanket behind. He held it tightly with one hand, and Bernard's present with the other, all the way to Bernard's house.

When they got there, Bernard's Mum opened the door.
"Hello, Alfie," she said. "Let's go into the garden
and find Bernard and the others."

Then Mum gave Alfie a kiss and said good-bye,
and went off to the park with Annie Rose.

"Would you like to put your blanket down here with the coats?" asked Bernard's Mum. But Alfie didn't want to put his blanket down. He still held on to it very tightly.

Bernard was in the garden with Min and Sam and Daniel and some other children from the Nursery School.

"Happy birthday!" Alfie remembered to say, and he gave Bernard his present. Bernard pulled off the paper.

"Crayons! How lovely!" said Bernard's Mum. "Say thank you, Bernard."

"Thank you," said Bernard. But do you know what he did then?

He threw the crayons up in the air. They landed all over the grass.

"That was a silly thing to do," said Bernard's Mum, as she picked up the crayons and put them away.

Then Bernard's Mum brought out some bubble stuff
and blew lots of bubbles into the air. They floated all
over the garden and the children jumped about trying
to pop them.

Alfie couldn't pop many bubbles because he was holding
on to his blanket. But Bernard jumped about and pushed
and popped more bubbles than anyone else.

"Don't push people, Bernard," said Bernard's Mum sternly.

One huge bubble landed
lightly on Min's sleeve. It
stayed there, quivering and
shiny. Min smiled. She
stood very still.

Then Bernard came up behind her and popped the big bubble.

Min began to cry. Bernard's Mum was cross with Bernard and told him to say he was sorry.

"Never mind, we're going to have tea now, dear," she told Min. "Who would you like to sit next to?"

Min wanted to sit next to Alfie. She stopped crying and pulled her chair right up close to his.

For tea there were sandwiches and little sausages on sticks and crisps and jellies and a big iced cake with candles and "Happy Birthday, Bernard" written on it.

Bernard took a huge breath and blew out
all the candles at once – *Phoooooo!* Everyone
clapped and sang "Happy Birthday to You".

Then Bernard blew into his lemonade through his straw and made rude bubbling noises. He blew into his jelly, too, until his Mum took it away from him.

Alfie liked the tea . . . but holding on to his blanket made eating rather difficult. It got all mixed up with the jelly and crisps, and covered in sticky crumbs.

After tea, Bernard's Mum said that they were all going to play a game. But Bernard ran off and fetched his very best present. It was a tiger mask.

Bernard went behind a bush and came out wearing the mask and making terrible growling noises: "Grrr! Grrr, grrrr, GRRRR! ACHT!"

He went crawling round the garden,
sounding very fierce and frightening.

Min began to cry again. She clung on to
Alfie.

"Get up *at once*, Bernard," said Bernard's Mum. "It's not that kind of game. Now let's all stand in a circle, everyone, and join hands."

Bernard stopped growling, but he wouldn't take off his tiger mask. Instead he grabbed Alfie's hand to pull him into the circle.

Bernard's Mum tried to take Min's hand and bring her into the circle, too. But Min wouldn't hold anyone's hand but Alfie's. She went on crying. She cried and cried.

Then Alfie made a brave decision. He ran and put down his blanket, very carefully, in a safe place underneath the table.

Now he could hold Min's hand, too, as well as Bernard's.

Min stopped crying. She wasn't frightened of Bernard in his tiger mask now she was holding Alfie's hand.

She joined in the game and they all
danced round together, singing:

"Ring-a-ring-o'-roses
A pocket full of posies
A-tishoo, a-tishoo,
We all fall DOWN!"

Afterwards Alfie and Min joined in with some more games and ate ice-cream and pop-corn and bounced balloons with the others. Alfie had such a good time that his blanket stayed under the table until Mum and Annie Rose came to collect him.

"What a helpful guest you've been, Alfie," said Bernard's Mum, when Alfie thanked her and said good-bye. "Min wouldn't have enjoyed the party a bit without you. I *do* wish Bernard would learn to be helpful sometimes –

– Perhaps he will, one day."

On the way home, Alfie carried his
blanket in one hand and a balloon and a
packet of sweets in the other. His blanket
had got a bit messy at the party. It had been
rather in the way, too. Next time he thought
he might leave it safely at home, after all.

The House
That Jack Built

Jenny Stow

FRANCES LINCOLN

First published in Great Britain in 1992 by
Frances Lincoln Limited, 4 Torriano Mews,
Torriano Avenue, London NW5 2RZ

First paperback edition 1999

British Library Cataloguing in Publication Data available on request

ISBN 0-7112-0717-8 hardback
ISBN 0-7112-1455-7 paperback

Printed in Hong Kong

9 8 7 6 5 4 3 2 1

For Jack

This is the house that Jack built.

This is the malt
That lay in the house that Jack built.

This is the rat,
That ate the malt,
That lay in the house that Jack built.

This is the cat,
That killed the rat,
That ate the malt,
That lay in the house that Jack built.

This is the dog,
That worried the cat,
That killed the rat,
That ate the malt,
That lay in the house that Jack built.

This is the cow with the crumpled horn,
That tossed the dog,
That worried the cat,
That killed the rat,
That ate the malt,
That lay in the house that Jack built.

This is the maiden all forlorn,
That milked the cow with the crumpled horn,
That tossed the dog,
That worried the cat,
That killed the rat,
That ate the malt,
That lay in the house that Jack built.

This is the man all tattered and torn,
That kissed the maiden all forlorn,
That milked the cow with the crumpled horn,
That tossed the dog,
That worried the cat,
That killed the rat,
That ate the malt,
That lay in the house that Jack built.

This is the priest all shaven and shorn,
That married the man all tattered and torn,
That kissed the maiden all forlorn,
That milked the cow with the crumpled horn,
That tossed the dog,
That worried the cat,
That killed the rat,
That ate the malt,
That lay in the house that Jack built.

This is the cock that crowed in the morn,
That waked the priest all shaven and shorn,
That married the man all tattered and torn,
That kissed the maiden all forlorn,
That milked the cow with the crumpled horn,
That tossed the dog,
That worried the cat,
That killed the rat,
That ate the malt,
That lay in the house that Jack built.

This is the farmer sowing his corn,
That kept the cock that crowed in the morn,
That waked the priest all shaven and shorn,
That married the man all tattered and torn,
That kissed the maiden all forlorn,
That milked the cow with the crumpled horn,
That tossed the dog,
That worried the cat,
That killed the rat,
That ate the malt,
That lay in the house that Jack built.

This is the house that Jack built.

MORE PICTURE BOOKS IN PAPERBACK
FROM FRANCES LINCOLN

GROWING PAINS

Jenny Stow

Poor baby Shukudu! It's hard trying to be a rhinocerous when you have no horns!
"Horns take time to grow," says his mother. A story of patience and friendship,
humorously told and warmly illustrated.

Suitable for National Curriculum English – Reading, Key Stage 1
Scottish Guidelines English Language – Reading, Levels B and C

ISBN 0-7112-1036-5 £4.99

FIDDLE-I-FEE

Jakki Wood

An exuberant retelling of a well-known nursery rhyme that will have
children singing along in no time. Margaret Lion has arranged the accompanying
melody, based on a traditional folk song, for piano and guitar.

Suitable for National Curriculum English – Key Stage 1
Scottish Guidelines English Language – Reading, Level A

ISBN 0-7112-0860-3 £4.99

CATS SLEEP ANYWHERE

Eleanor Farjeon
Illustrated by Anne Mortimer

From an open drawer, to an empty shoe, on top of the piano or in an armchair,
as any cat lover knows, cats will sleep anywhere! Enchanting illustrations
by Anne Mortimer capture the elegance of this delightful poem.

Suitable for National Curriculum English – Reading, Speaking and Listening, Key Stages 1 and 2
Scottish Guidelines English Language – Reading, Talking and Listening, Level A

ISBN 0-7112-1286-4 £4.99

Frances Lincoln titles are available from all good bookshops.
Prices are correct at time of publication, but may be subject to change.